The Room Of Woe

by Rich Wallace
illustrated by Jose Emroca Flores

Calico

An Imprint of Magic Wagon
www.abdopublishing.com

www.abdopublishing.com

Published by Magic Wagon, a division of ABDO, PO Box 398166, Minneapolis, Minnesota 55439. Copyright © 2015 by Abdo Consulting Group, Inc. International copyrights reserved in all countries. No part of this book may be reproduced in any form without written permission from the publisher. Calico™ is a trademark and logo of Magic Wagon.

Printed in the United States of America, North Mankato, Minnesota.
102014
012015

THIS BOOK CONTAINS RECYCLED MATERIALS

Written by Rich Wallace
Illustrations by Jose Emroca Flores
Edited by Heidi M. D. Elston, Megan Gunderson, Bridget O'Brien
Cover and interior design by Laura Rask

Library of Congress Cataloging-in-Publication Data

Wallace, Rich, author.
  The room of Woe : an Up2U horror adventure / by Rich Wallace ; illustrated by Jose Emroca Flores.
      pages cm. -- (Up2U adventures)
  Summary: Max is not keen about staying at his Aunt Ida's house, and when the ghost of her long-dead son, Woe, begins to torment him he decides to take his chances on the nearby mountain, even though it is night--but the ghost pursues him, and how the adventure ends is up to the reader to choose.
  ISBN 978-1-62402-094-0
1. Ghost stories. 2. Plot-your-own stories. 3. Horror tales. 4. Haunted houses--Juvenile fiction. [1. Ghosts--Fiction. 2. Haunted houses--Fiction. 3. Horror stories. 4. Plot-your-own stories.] I. Emroca Flores, Jose, illustrator. II. Title.
PZ7.W15877Rr 2015
813.54--dc23
[Fic]
                                    2014034275

TABLE OF CONTENTS

CHAPTER
→ 1 ←

Butcher Mountain

I had an uneasy feeling about spending two days at Aunt Ida's house. She's strange. Always pinching my ears and telling me what a handsome boy I am.

"She's totally harmless," my father said. "You'll be fine."

We'd left our house only a few minutes earlier. My parents had already told me at least five times I'd be fine. Of course, that made me more certain I wouldn't be.

I looked out the car window as we passed the bank and the frozen yogurt shop. In one more minute, we were out of town.

"You'll be in good hands, Max," Dad said. "It's only for a couple of days."

Mom giggled. "I admit Aunt Ida is a little odd. But Dad and I will be there at night. You'll have nothing to worry about during the day, right?"

I nodded. Neither of them saw that though, since I was in the backseat.

We were already in the woods, driving toward the state park. Mom had decided this bird-watching trip was urgent. Some of their birding friends had spotted a rare little songbird in the forest on Butcher Mountain. Or, at least, someone thought they had. My parents couldn't resist checking for themselves.

They also kept assuring me I had nothing to worry about.

"You've been to Aunt Ida's house," Dad said. "It's very peaceful. The stream, the forest, and that incredible view of the mountain."

I did not recall that I'd ever been to Aunt Ida's home. She lives way outside of town. She's my grandma's oldest sister, but we only see her a few times a year. She always comes to our house for Thanksgiving, birthdays, or cookouts. We never go there.

"She's very excited to see you," Mom said. "Look, she sent me this e-mail to show you."

Mom handed me her tablet, and I read the message.

Dear Max,
I am delighted that we'll be spending a
couple of days together. You'll share
Woe's room while you are here.
Fondly,
Aunt Ida

"Who is Woe?" I asked. No one had ever mentioned him.

Mom and Dad looked at each other. Then Dad fixed his gaze on the road.

"Worthington was my cousin," Mom said. "He was quite a lot older than me. I never knew him. He died before I was born."

"Then why does he have a room at Aunt Ida's house?"

"Well," Mom said, "Ida only had one child. So I guess no one else ever needed the room. She kept it the way it was."

"She just calls it Woe's room," Dad said, trying to explain. "Because it was his."

Mom smiled and said something she probably thought would sound exciting, but she just made it worse. "You'll probably be the first kid to sleep there since . . ." I knew what she was about to say.

Dad let out his breath in a big sigh. He finished Mom's thought for her. "You'll be the first to sleep there in a long time," he said.

We followed Route 101 for about fifteen more minutes. Nobody said anything, but I was thinking hard.

"Did Worthington die in that room?" I finally asked.

"No," Dad said. "No, no, no."

"What happened to him?"

They glanced at each other again. Then Dad turned onto a narrow dirt road beside a lake.

"He fell," Mom said.

"He fell?"

"He fell off a cliff."

"A long time ago," Dad added.

"Before I was born," Mom repeated.

I could see a small white house up ahead. It was barely visible in the thick pine trees and the shadow of Butcher Mountain. The mountain rose to a flat peak. It was the highest mountain in the area, though it wasn't huge.

"How old was he?" I asked.

"A year or so younger than you are now," Mom said. "He was ten."

"And when did he die?"

"About fifty years ago."

Mom lowered her window. "Listen," she said. "Maybe we'll hear the vireo."

The bird they'd be seeking was a white-eyed vireo. It's supposed to be rare this far north in New England, but not unheard of. Neither of my parents had ever seen one. The car was loaded with their backpacks, binoculars, hiking boots, and cameras.

"What does it sound like?" I asked. I didn't care much about birds, but I didn't have much else to do this weekend.

"Chip-a-whee," Mom said. "Chip-a-*wheeeee*."

The car bounced to a stop under a giant white pine tree. The air smelled damp, like kicked-up mud. The house was entirely in the shade.

Aunt Ida's house was the last one on the dead-end road, and there were no others in sight. The side door was open. I could see the kitchen through the screen.

"The April birding season is so exciting," Mom said. "You can still join us if you want, Max."

I shook my head. I'd take my chances with Aunt Ida. I had a couple of books with me, and my parents had promised there were lots of old toys at Ida's house.

"Just don't stay out in the woods too late," I said. "This place looks like it'll be creepy after dark."

Mom laughed. Dad did, too, but his laugh didn't sound convincing.

Aunt Ida swung open the screen door and stepped out. She had her arms wide and a big grin on her face.

"Welcome!" Ida said. "Such a pleasure to see you." She hugged me with those bony arms, then tugged my ear. Mom and Dad were already putting on their backpacks and floppy hats.

"We'll be home before dark," Mom said. "But we need to get started. If there's only one white-eyed vireo in this forest, he won't be easy to find."

"Can't you stay a few minutes first?" Ida asked. "I made sandwiches. Tuna fish with olives."

"We packed a lunch," Dad said. "Max loves tuna fish, though. He'll gobble it up."

"Yes," Ida said. "He's a growing boy." She patted my shoulder and led me toward the house. I watched my parents stomp off into the woods. They were out of sight in seconds.

The house was small and square. There was only the kitchen, a narrow living room, and a bedroom on the ground floor.

"Go on in," Ida said, pointing to the bedroom. "I'll serve your lunch in there. You two can get to know each other."

"Two?" I asked.

"Oh, yes," Aunt Ida replied. "Worthington can't wait to meet you."

CHAPTER
→» 2 «←

Pieces of the Puzzle

Woe's room was small and neat, with a
bookcase lining one wall. The windows looked
out on the wooded slope. Bins of plastic soldiers
and dinosaurs sat near the foot of the bed. Puzzles
and cards were piled in a corner, and small wooden
alphabet blocks stood in a neat stack.

The most interesting item in the room was an
old record player. A shiny record about the size of
a dinner plate sat on the turntable. The record's
label said "Mairzy Doats" by the Merry Macs.

I knelt down, plugged in the player, and turned
a switch. The record began spinning, and I set the
needle so it would play.

The record was scratchy and the words made no sense at all: "Mairzy doats and dozy doats . . ."

The floor squeaked behind me.

"Oh, Worthington loves that song," Ida said as she entered. She set down a tray with two plates and two glasses. "He already had his lunch, so I just brought crackers for him. And iced tea for you both."

I stared at my sandwich. It looked good.

Ida took a sip of the iced tea. Then she popped one of the crackers into her mouth.

"I'll be upstairs sewing," she said, turning to leave. "Have fun. Get to know each other."

I sipped from the other glass. The record was skipping, so I shut it off.

There was another sound. A steady *ping-ping-ping*. It took a moment before I realized a heavy rain was blowing against the window.

Maybe the rain would drive my parents back to the house. Probably not. The chance to add

a new bird to their ledger would keep them out in any storm.

My eyes fixed on an old photograph in a silver frame. It was a boy about my age. His glare looked mean. It was Worthington, for sure. He was blond and was wearing a thin necktie. Probably a school portrait.

Worthington's stare was creepy. I was still on my knees, so I hobbled over to the bookcase to pick up the picture. His gaze seemed to follow me in the gloomy light.

I sat against the wall and ate my sandwich, which was tasty and filling. I thought about eating a cracker to make Aunt Ida happy. She could pretend Worthington had eaten it.

An old red book caught my eye, so I pulled it from the shelf. It was a picture book for little kids, but it was one of my favorites: *Mike Mulligan and His Steam Shovel*. I read the whole thing.

Aunt Ida came back as I finished the book. "You're a good eater," she said, picking up my empty plate. She tilted her head toward the tray. "I guess Woe wasn't so hungry. I'll leave this for later." She picked up another cracker and took a bite. "These are so good," she said. "But salty." She helped herself to another gulp of "Woe's" iced tea.

Ida walked out, closing the door behind her. I couldn't help but laugh after she left the room. It was kind of sad Ida pretended Worthington was still here, half a century after he died. But it was a little funny, too. Losing him must have been very hard. I could tell she'd never gotten over it. Making believe he was here must help soothe the pain.

The rain grew harder, and the wind rattled the shutters. The windowpane was fogged up. There was no way a vireo would be flying around in this storm.

I picked up a puzzle box and shook it. There were bound to be some missing pieces, but I'd make do. I dumped the cardboard pieces onto the wood floor and started sorting them.

I worked on it for an hour. The puzzle began to take shape. It showed several boats on a lake, with a dock in the foreground. I pieced together the fourth corner and sorted through the remaining pieces.

Three pieces fit together, but they didn't seem to match any spot in the grid. I found a fourth and locked it to the others, forming a face.

The face was exactly like Worthington's from the portrait!

Aunt Ida knocked on the door at the same time the face appeared. I jumped. "I have to run out for a short while," Ida said. "I'm just going to the store," she said. "I might be gone an hour."

"All right," I replied, my voice squeaking.

I opened the bedroom door and wondered if I should go with her. But the rain was heavy, so I decided to stay.

"We need more crackers," Ida said. She stepped into the room and ate the final cracker on the plate. "He loves them. See? All gone."

"All gone," I repeated.

I watched Ida back her car onto the dirt road and drive away. The shutters rattled some more. I think I even heard thunder.

I wandered into the kitchen.

The refrigerator was well stocked. I took an apple, then walked up the creaky stairs to look around.

Upstairs, there were two bedrooms and a bathroom. Aunt Ida's room was crowded with blankets and floor lamps and stacks of books.

The other one had just a bed and a small dresser. It looked as if no one ever went in there.

I heard music playing from somewhere. It was slightly familiar. I walked slowly down the stairs and shivered when I realized what the song was.

"Mairzy Doats." It was coming from Worthington's room. I knew I had turned it off.

The record started skipping again, and I unplugged it this time. I looked around for any clue to how it had started, but I found nothing unusual.

But then I looked at the window.

Words were forming on the fogged-up glass, as if someone was writing with a finger.

The writing said, *Get out of my room.*

CHAPTER

3

Flying Objects

The front door swung open as I rushed out of the bedroom. Dad was shaking like a wet dog, sneezing and wiping his eyes.

I took a deep breath, trying to hide how scared I was.

"Any luck?" I asked.

"Just bad luck," Dad replied. "It's too stormy to find anything."

"No it isn't," Mom said. "The vireo is out there somewhere, I know it."

Dad patted his hair with a towel. "That bird could be a hundred miles away from here by now," he said. "If it was ever here. And that's a big if. *If* it was ever here, it's probably long gone by now."

"I think I heard it an hour ago," Mom said. "I heard a chirpy 'chip-a.' Not quite a 'chip-a-whee,' but something like it."

Dad shook his head slowly. "We're not even in its normal range."

"Its range has been expanding every year," Mom said. "The northern edge of its confirmed range is less than twenty miles from here. It's very likely the white-eyed vireo has already moved into this region."

This was a common way for my parents to interact. Mom was always open to new possibilities. Dad usually was not. He wouldn't believe the bird was here until he saw it with his own eyes.

"Let's build a fire," he said. "I'm soaked and freezing."

There was newspaper and kindling in a pile by the fireplace. I went outside and grabbed some bigger pieces of wood. They were wet, but Dad used them anyway. The wood sizzled and steamed, but soon we had a cozy fire.

I settled into the couch and felt warm. Having my parents back made the house seem less sinister. I decided my imagination had gone out of control. I hadn't seen Worthington's face in the puzzle pieces or read his writing on the window, right? It was just my imagination and fear.

Aunt Ida roasted a chicken for dinner, and we ate ice cream for dessert. The adults taught me how to play a card game as the wind howled and the rain came down in sheets.

So I wasn't feeling scared at bedtime. They'd all be right upstairs. The house was warm and secure. A good sleep was all I needed.

Mom came into the room after I'd climbed into bed. She was carrying a field guide, with pictures of birds and maps of their habitats.

"Here's our quarry," she said, showing me a picture of the white-eyed vireo. It had a yellowish head and belly, with olive-colored wings. "These little guys are very secretive, but we'll find one tomorrow. I just know it."

"Dad's not so sure about that," I said.

Mom winked. "I'm sure," she said. "I know my birds. The thickets on this hillside are perfect for vireos."

I lay awake for more than an hour, listening to the house creak in the wind. It was a soothing sound, especially since my parents were upstairs. I would have felt different if I were alone. Or if just Aunt Ida had been here.

I fell into a deep sleep, so I don't know what time it was when I woke up. The room was pitch dark, but I felt a sharp object poking into my back. I rolled over and swept my hand across the sheet. It hit something hard. I grabbed my flashlight from the side table.

It was one of the plastic dinosaurs. Its pointy horns had been jabbing into me. I tossed it into the bin with the other toys and got back in bed.

I fell asleep again. Then I rolled over and jumped as I came into contact with a small metal tractor. Why had someone left all these toys in the bed?

I pulled back the cover and made sure there weren't any more toys. Then I lay awake for a long time again, staring at the ceiling.

And then I heard the record scratching.

"Mairzy doats and dozy doats . . ."

I leaped out of bed and unplugged the record player again. Aunt Ida must have plugged it in. But why had it started up? Maybe the storm had caused a short in the electric system.

I sat on the floor in the dark, confused and afraid. Something hit my arm. Then my head. Playing cards were floating down from the ceiling. A whole deck of them!

"This is nuts," I whispered.

Then I heard a *thunk.*

Several alphabet blocks flew out of the bed and hit the wall above me. A handful of plastic soldiers followed. The bedcovers rustled, and I inched back against the wall and stared in disbelief. Someone was definitely in the bed.

The door opened and my dad poked his head in. I shined my light at him.

"Max?"

"Here."

"Why are you playing so late at night?"

"Uh . . . I couldn't sleep."

"Well, tone it down. Stop throwing toys around. The rest of us need to sleep."

"Okay, Dad."

"You can play or read until you get sleepy, but keep it quiet, pal."

I heard every step squeak as he made his way back upstairs.

When I looked back at the bed, I saw a blond head sticking out of the covers. Worthington was glaring at me. He was glowing green. I turned the light beam toward him, and he disappeared.

I felt as if I were frozen to the floor. Would Worthington attack me if I moved? Would he keep me from leaving the room? Where had he gone? Was he invisible now? I shined the light around the room, trying to find him. I didn't see him. Not seeing him was worse than seeing him, though. I wanted to know where he was so I could keep away from him.

My heart was pounding, and my hands were shaky. I pressed my back against the wall and took a few deep breaths.

I looked at the bed. The covers were flat. There was no sign anyone was in the bed now. I swept the room with the beam again, and everything seemed still.

There was no way I was getting back into that bed. I crawled out to the living room and huddled under an old blanket on the couch.

A little while later, I heard "Mairzy Doats" playing again. And then I heard a laugh. From that bedroom. It didn't sound like a happy laugh at all.

I didn't sleep another second all night. I just shivered under the blanket with the flashlight on until I saw the first streaks of dawn.

CHAPTER
→ 4 ←

At Rest

I heard the adults moving around upstairs, so I tiptoed back to my bedroom at daybreak. I didn't want them knowing I'd sat on the couch all night. I don't like to show fear.

Toys were scattered about the room. The record player was still unplugged, and the bed was rumpled but empty.

The photo of Worthington looked normal in the morning light. I touched the frame, and a yellowed piece of newspaper fell out of the frame. I unfolded it and read. It was dated June 14, 1963.

Missing Climber Found Dead

Park rangers have recovered the body of 10-year-old Worthington Bedford, who apparently tumbled from a cliff on Thursday evening off Butcher Mountain. The boy was pronounced dead at the scene.

Officials said Worthington became lost while on a late-afternoon hike and fell to his death after dark. He had been alone, but he was familiar with most of the trails. He lived with his mother on Harris Road at the base of the mountain.

I heard footsteps and held the newspaper clipping behind my back. Aunt Ida came in with a plate of toast and two cups of orange juice.

"Good morning!" she said in a cheery voice. "Sleep well?"

"Yes," I lied, but I couldn't stop myself from yawning.

"Well, you two can start with this rye toast. I'll make a real breakfast when your parents come down."

Ida took a big bite of toast. "Just right," she said as she chewed. "Woe doesn't care for much butter on his." She washed it down with half the orange juice.

"No trouble during the night?" she asked.

I shook my head and glanced at Worthington's photo. "The record player seemed to start by itself once. Has that ever happened before?"

"No," Ida replied. She bent to look at the record. "That's Worthington's favorite song. Such silly lyrics. He plays it all the time."

"Dozy doats," I said.

"Exactly. Well, I'll leave you be. The pancakes will be ready soon." She took another bite of toast and drank most of the remaining orange juice.

I slid the newspaper clipping into the back of the frame.

The rain had stopped sometime during the night, but the wind was still up and everything was damp and cold outside. It wasn't springlike at all.

My parents talked about the vireo while we ate our pancakes. Dad was in a better mood this morning. He agreed they'd be more likely to find the bird if the rain held up.

We walked the grounds after breakfast. Mom was eager to get out into the woods, but Dad said they should spend a few minutes with me first. He pointed out a warbler's nest in a gnarled old apple tree.

We walked down the hill a short way. There was a small family burial plot on a ridge below the house. Hemlocks and pines kept it in shade. There were five grave sites. The ones for Ida's mother and father and her husband and brother were neat and orderly, with flowers growing nearby. A smaller headstone off to the side was overgrown with weeds. I pushed some of the growth away to read it.

WORTHINGTON BEDFORD
September 7, 1952–June 13, 1963
At Rest

My parents had wandered off down the slope, but Ida was standing behind me.

"He doesn't need it yet," she said.

I wasn't sure what she meant. I guess my look told her that.

"Worthington," she said. "He's not ready to be there."

I nodded. I'd seen proof of that last night.

"I'm glad he has a playmate this weekend," Ida said.

Playmate? I seemed to be someone for him to torment.

Darker clouds were rolling in. Another stormy day ahead. Mom walked quickly toward the house with Dad dragging behind. "Let's go!" she said.

Within a minute they were heading out on the trail.

"Chip-a-whee!" I called.

"Chip-a-whee!" Mom called back.

Things were quiet for most of the day. I stayed in the living room and kept a fire going while I read a book. Ida went in and out of Woe's room a few times with cups of juice and plates of crackers or a sandwich. The rain was on and off. My parents stayed out all day, not returning for lunch.

It was nearly six o'clock when Ida announced she was going to the store again. "Worthington ate an entire box of crackers today," she said with a goofy smile. She shook the empty box to show me. "I'll be back in an hour or so."

I wondered why she didn't buy two or three boxes of crackers at a time, since "Woe" ate so many.

As soon as her car was out of sight, that toy metal tractor came bumping down the steps. *Crunk. Crunk. Crunk.*

Then a closet door slammed upstairs. *Bam*.

The record player started up again, this time at full volume. But it wasn't the same song. I poked my head into the room and looked around. All seemed calm except for the music.

I took a deep breath and unplugged the record player. The record had been flipped to its B side, which read "I Got 10 Bucks and 24 Hours Leave," also by the Merry Macs. I carefully set the record down. I felt a sudden sharp pain in my thigh as a block fell to the floor. I dodged as another one came flying toward my head.

"Stop it, Woe!" I yelled, but the blocks kept coming. Books flew off the shelf and came at me, and a strong, cold breeze pushed me toward the door.

I grabbed my flashlight and raced out of the room. I stepped into my sneakers and ran from the house, hoping the rain had stopped. It had. Luckily I was wearing a sweatshirt. I ran to the edge of the woods, tied my sneakers, and took off along the path to try to find my parents.

The shadows were long and dark, and I knew there wasn't much more than an hour of daylight left. If I stayed on the main trail, I would probably meet up with my parents as they headed back.

I could holler for them, but it would be my luck to scare off that rare vireo just when they had it cornered. So I kept quiet and alert. I figured I was safe as long as I stayed away from that house.

But I wanted to get as far away as I could. And I'd never go back there again.

CHAPTER

→» 5 «←

Stalked

The old pine needles underfoot were springy, but the trail was soggy from all that rain. Birds were chirping. None of them sounded like a vireo.

The trail forked, and I took the path that went up. My gut told me my parents would have climbed toward the peak. I went as fast as I could, but there were lots of roots and large stones.

Please be on your way down, Mom and Dad, I thought. *Get me out of this place.*

The rain held off, but every time the wind gusted I got splashed with water from the trees. My sneakers were soaked through, and my sweatshirt was getting wet, too.

It was soon dark enough that I needed the flashlight. The beam was very weak. The batteries weren't fresh. And the flashlight had been on all night.

Come on, Mom. Time to go, Dad.

I looked back when I reached another fork. Fifty yards away, I saw a flash of blond. Was Worthington following me?

I walked faster.

My heart was pumping harder than ever. I felt chilled to the bone.

Maybe it wasn't him. Maybe I'd caught a glimpse of a deer. It was hard to tell in the fading light. I wasn't waiting around to find out.

I reached a small clearing with a view over the valley. I couldn't see any roads or houses. But I could see up. The peak was a long way off.

Dad had told me you could see Aunt Ida's house from the peak. If I could get up there, I could figure out a way down.

I listened hard, hoping to hear my parents. There were so many trails on this mountain. It would take a lot of luck to find them.

My stomach rumbled. I hadn't eaten since noon. I was panting from all the climbing, too. I was tired and thirsty. A big yawn escaped. I hadn't slept much at all the night before.

And I was certain I was being followed.

There were black bears on this mountain, but they didn't bother people. Usually. They'd be hungry this time of year, though, having slept most of the winter. Food was still scarce. No berries yet. Bears would be out looking hard for food.

But I knew it wasn't a bear.

I looked back every few feet. I'd see movement behind the pines. Maybe a flash of blond hair. I kept walking. Fast. I shouldn't be afraid of a ten-year-old kid. But who knew what a dead one could do?

"Mom!" I finally called. If they hadn't found that vireo by now, they never would. "Dad! Where are you?"

There was no answer. Maybe I heard an echo of my voice.

The only thing I could think of was to get to the top of the mountain. The top was sort of flat and clear of trees. I'd be able to see a great distance all around. That was my best hope of getting down again.

I'd already lost sight of how to get back. Maybe my parents were at the house, wondering where I was.

Come find me, I thought. *I'm doomed out here on my own!*

I turned around. I didn't see anything moving behind me. I didn't hear footsteps. I let out my breath. I rested.

And I wondered if I'd get off this mountain before daybreak.

Or at all.

I remembered that news clipping. Worthington "fell to his death after dark. He had been alone, but he was familiar with most of the trails."

I wasn't familiar with *any* of these trails. The odds of my getting out of here safely weren't good.

So I kept climbing.

And worrying.

The forest sounded deathly quiet now. No more chirping. Even the wind had stopped.

"Mom! Dad!"

Silence.

I leaned against a boulder.

And then I heard a laugh. It wasn't an adult. It was the same laugh I'd heard last night. A laugh from a small boy.

There was nothing funny about it.

My sense of direction is not great. I couldn't tell where the laugh came from, and I also could not tell which way I'd walked. The only direction I was sure of was *up*. So I started climbing again. Slowly, because I couldn't see very well. The only light now was the weak beam of the flashlight. I hoped it would last a few hours more.

"Mom! Dad?"

The only reply was another creepy giggle. Worthington was stalking me. What would he do if he caught me?

The trees grew thinner as I climbed, but the trail got steeper. Suddenly there was light up ahead. For a second, I thought I'd been found.

The moon had peeked out from behind the clouds. It was nearly full, and it cast a glow over part of the mountain. I could see it would soon be covered in clouds again. They were moving fast.

I took advantage of the moonlight and scrambled up the hill as quickly as I could. The peak was still several hundred yards ahead, but I knew I could get there. I knew I could find a way down if I reached the top.

The clouds covered the moon. It was as if a light had burned out. But I'd made some progress. The peak wasn't far ahead now.

Keep going, I told myself. *You're almost there.*

And then I got hit in the shoulder with an alphabet block.

A second one whizzed past my head. A third whacked my hand.

I ducked behind a boulder and held my breath. Another block landed nearby. I shut off the flashlight. Could he still see me?

I heard Worthington laughing, but the blocks stopped flying.

"I'll find you," came his voice. "You can't hide from me all night!"

I stayed still for what seemed like an hour. The moon went in and out of the clouds. Each time it shone, I huddled closer to the stone.

"Come on out," Worthington called. "I'd never hurt you." Then he laughed. His laugh sounded evil.

I clung to the boulder. My teeth were chattering as much from fear as from cold. And my

hands were shaking and numb. I wouldn't let him know where I was.

But I couldn't stay here all night. I'd die from the wet and the cold.

I had to get down from this mountain.

And the only way to get down was to go up.

CHAPTER
→ 6 ←

Freezing and Lost

You would think that with such outdoorsy parents I would have developed better survival skills. They'd taught me a lot of things about hiking and camping over the years:

Always tell someone where you are going.

Be sure to have a good flashlight with fresh batteries.

Bring water and a snack.

Have proper clothing for cold, rain, snow, you name it.

Know the area you'll be going to. Bring a trail map.

I hadn't done any of those things.

Then again, they'd never mentioned what to do if you're fleeing from an angry ghost. If I'd taken time to pack a sandwich and an umbrella, Worthington might have plunked me over the head with a frying pan. I had to get out of that house as fast as I could.

"Mom!" I yelled. "Daaaaaad!"

There was no reply. Then I heard Worthington's teasing voice.

"Mommy," he whined. "Daddy."

That got me mad. I was still scared out of my wits, but a little bit of anger felt good. I yelled for my parents again.

Worthington laughed.

I kept climbing, grabbing branches to help me up the steep slope. My feet were slipping in the mud and the loose gravel. But I was getting close to the peak.

Climb, I told myself. *Don't look back.*

But when I looked up, I saw him.

Worthington was at the top of the mountain, just fifty yards ahead. He was glowing slightly, as he had last night in his bedroom. Like an eerie green halo. The moon broke through again. Worthington disappeared. The light from the moon was brighter than he was.

I could see stars now, too. The last of the clouds were moving quickly away. The top of the mountain was clear to me. No more trees. There was just a little more of the rocky slope to cover.

I almost felt safe for the first time in hours. It was cold at the top, but now I could get my bearings. Slowly I turned a full circle, looking for the lights of a house or a road down below.

"Hello!" I shouted as loud as I could. "Mom? Dad? I'm on top of Butcher Mountain!"

No answer.

"Help! Anybody!"

There was no response except a faraway giggle.

And I couldn't see any signs of life in the valley.

No lights. No cars.

Nothing.

"Hey!" I screamed. But all I heard was an echo.

I closed my eyes and slowly shook my head. The wind up here was strong and cold. I had to get down. But which way?

The mountaintop was a small, flat area, about the size of a baseball diamond. There were some boulders off to the side. I carefully climbed one, and I could see farther.

Success! I saw a small pattern of lights far below that looked like three or four houses. They wouldn't be Aunt Ida's, but it didn't matter now. As long as I could get to a house, I could call my parents. But this side of the mountain looked very steep and dangerous. I would have to circle around.

I slid off the boulder and looked for a trail to follow. Everything away from the mountaintop was very dark. The trees kept the moonlight from shining through.

It was too severe up here. I couldn't stay. So I chose a direction and started toward the woods.

Climbing up a mountain is hard, but going down in the dark is even harder. I slipped several times before I'd gone a hundred yards. The flashlight was almost worthless now. Its beam made only a small, faint circle in front of me.

But then I saw another glow. I stopped short. The glow turned green, and it began to take shape.

It was Worthington! He was smiling at me and pointing to a trail on the right. Would that trail lead me to Aunt Ida's house? Or would it send me over the cliff where he'd fallen so many years before?

"Just follow me," Worthington said. "We can be friends. Forever."

How? If I became a ghost, too?

I stood still for a long time, wondering what to do. Worthington kept pointing. Maybe he would lead me to safety. Maybe he'd lead me to my death.

Just behind Worthington, the trail split into two. The path to the left seemed more likely to lead to those houses. My gut told me I should go left.

"This is the way," Worthington said, pointing to the right again.

I had a third choice, too. If I refused to follow Worthington, he'd probably go back to Aunt Ida's house. Perhaps I could follow him secretly.

"Come along, Max," Worthington said. "I wouldn't lead you wrong."

Yes, you would.

But I was freezing. Hungry. Lost.

I had to make a decision now.

My life depended on it.

The Ending Is Up2U!

If you think Max should trust Worthington
and follow him on the path to the right,
turn to page 54.

→ OR ←

If you think it would be a better idea for
Max to trust his gut instinct and take the path
to the left, turn to page 64.

→ OR ←

If you think Max should pretend to ignore
Worthington but secretly try to follow him
home, turn to page 72.

ENDING

→ 1 ←

Trusting Woe

I didn't really trust Worthington, but following his lead seemed like my best choice. He must know every inch of that mountain after fifty years. He wouldn't make the same deadly mistake twice.

Or would he? He was already dead. Maybe his plan was to kill me, too. Was that what he meant when he said we could be friends "forever"?

"All right, Worthington," I said. "Take me home." I'd watch the trail very carefully. If I sensed any danger, I would stop.

Worthington grinned and started to float toward the woods. He was easy to follow with his greenish glow, so I stayed several yards behind.

We edged along a banked trail, then came out onto open ground at the side of the mountain.

"It's very steep here," Worthington said.

With the moonlight, I could see a big drop to my right. It was too dark to see how far it was to the bottom. Stones fell away from my sneakers. A couple of seconds passed before I heard them hit.

It was far enough to crush me if I fell.

Why was Worthington being nice to me all of a sudden? To build up my trust so he could lead me to an even steeper fall?

I walked very slowly, as if on a tightrope. The path was wide enough, but one bad step could send me over the edge.

I began to sweat. That was a good sign. At least I wasn't freezing. But I sure didn't feel warm. Most of the sweat was from fear.

We reached safer ground. The trail dropped quickly, and soon we were back in the deep, dark woods.

"Worthington?" I called.

He stopped and turned. I couldn't see his full body. Just his head and shoulders were clear. The rest of him was a mist.

"What?" he replied.

"Was that where you died?"

"Back there? No. I never go near *that* cliff. No, that was just a steep drop-off back there."

"You never go back there?"

"Only that one time."

I began to feel bad for Worthington. He'd been dead for fifty years. But he was still stuck here on Earth.

"What do you do all day?" I asked.

"Play. Listen to music. Watch over my mother."

"*You* watch over *her*?"

"Yes," he said. "I'm all she has." With that, he turned and moved quickly down the mountain. I tried to keep up.

"Slow down!" I called. "I can't see well."

I followed him down a slippery slope, leaning into trees to keep from tumbling.

"Are we getting close to home?" I asked.

Worthington did not reply.

I stumbled and landed on my knees. My hand hit a rock and began to bleed. Branches scratched my face when I rose.

"How much farther?" I asked.

Worthington finally stopped. "It's a big mountain," he said. "We still have a ways to go."

I knew there were much bigger mountains than this. But it might be the only one he'd ever seen.

"Will you come back to visit me?" Worthington asked.

"Never!" I said. "I don't ever want to go through this again."

Worthington suddenly turned the color of fire. Sparks and smoke flew from his head. He looked very angry. I knew I had said the wrong thing.

"I've been alone for fifty years!" he hollered. "You're the first one near my age to visit in all that time. Why wouldn't you come back to visit if I saved your life?"

"I will!" I cried. My whole body was shaking. "Just get me off this mountain safely and I promise I'll return."

Worthington's color slowly returned to the greenish glow. He nodded, but he still looked angry. "This way," he said, pointing to a new trail. "Follow me."

I gulped. Was this the trail to the cliff? I stayed still for a moment, wondering what to do.

Worthington kept going.

Careful, I told myself. *Take your time.*

I followed Worthington again.

The trail was steep, but we didn't seem to be near any cliff. Instead, we cut through the forest and wound back and forth. Each step got us closer to the bottom.

I felt safer. But I kept my guard up.

"Do you listen to that same record every day?" I asked. "That silly 'Mairzy Doats' song?"

"It's the only one we have," he said.

There was a music store near our house. It mostly sold used CDs and tapes. I had seen some old records in there once. I'd get some "new" ones for Woe. Listening to that record every day for fifty years must have been torture.

"And do you really eat any of those crackers?"

"Of course not," he said. "I'm a ghost."

My throat was feeling dry and tight. I'd had nothing to drink for a long while. The thirst was greater than my hunger, but I would have eaten a whole box of those crackers if I had the chance.

We circled around a large boulder. The breeze picked up. I thought I heard a voice down below.

Worthington and I both froze.

"Max!" That was definitely my dad.

Worthington flashed orange again. More sparks flew into the air.

"Over here!" I yelled.

"Stay where you are!" Dad called. "We'll come to you!"

I could already see their lights, bobbing as they climbed toward us.

Worthington faded quickly. I could barely see him. "Will you visit me again?" he asked. He sounded very sad.

"Yes," I said. "I promise I will."

He winked and waved, and with that, he was gone.

"Here I am!" I called. I raised my flashlight overhead and waved it. The beam was so weak that it cast almost no light.

"We're almost there!" Mom called. "Stay still, Max. I love you!"

I sat on the wet ground and waited. I was shivering again, but I didn't care.

In just a few seconds I'd be with my parents. In an hour I'd be home, at my own house, showered and warm and safe.

The beams from their flashlights reached me. Mom hugged me tight. Dad did, too.

"What happened?" they both asked.

I started to speak, but stopped. Would anyone believe me? "I wanted to see if I could find that bird," I finally said. "I didn't plan to go far. But every trail looked the same."

Dad helped me into his rain jacket and hat. Mom handed me a water bottle, and I drank the entire thing.

We didn't have far to go. In ten minutes, I could see Aunt Ida's house.

"Did you find that vireo?" I asked.

"We heard it," Mom said. "But never quite saw it."

"Beautiful sound," Dad said. "But the only sight we cared about tonight was you."

Aunt Ida insisted we eat dinner at her house, so we did. It didn't seem so scary now. I put on dry clothing.

After we ate, I went back into Woe's room. Everything looked the same. The toys were neatly put away. The photo was propped up on the bookcase.

I nodded at the picture. Was Woe my cousin or my uncle? It didn't matter. He was my relative. After a rough start, he'd helped me get to safety.

"See you next time, Woe," I whispered. "I promise it won't be long."

ENDING

→» 2 «←

Finding My Own Way

Worthington had thrown blocks and books at me, jabbed me with a dinosaur horn, and done all he could to scare me out of Aunt Ida's house. There was no way I would trust him. I'd rather keep trying to find my own way down the mountain.

If I followed Worthington, he would probably lead me right off the cliff.

"Leave me alone," I told him. I pointed to the trail on the left. "I'm going that way."

"You'll be sorry," he said.

I did wonder why no one seemed to be searching for me. I'd left the house two hours earlier. My parents must have returned from bird-watching by now. Maybe they were on their way up to find me.

"Mom! Dad!"

There was no response. Then Worthington laughed.

"Go away," I said. I walked, shining my weak flashlight beam on the trail to the left.

It didn't matter which trail I took, as long as I stayed safe. Any trail that went down the mountain would eventually get me there. Even if I came out miles away from Aunt Ida's, I could find a house and call my parents.

But avoiding a fall was hard. I kept slipping on muddy slopes and gravel. I could see only a few yards in front of me.

Something small was moving on the path. A snake? I focused the light on it.

It was a plastic soldier! It was about three inches tall, just like the ones in Woe's room. My light showed there were several more, marching in a line. How did Worthington do that?

The soldiers stopped. It looked as if each one was pointing to my right. Then they started marching again.

Probably toward the cliff.

Did Worthington think he could fool me like that? Not a chance. I kept going in the same direction I'd been headed.

The soldiers followed me. They seemed to be singing! I bent low to hear.

They were singing "Mairzy Doats"!

I felt a chill. If Worthington could control plastic soldiers like that, what could he do to me?

"Mom!" I yelled. "Dad!"

I heard Worthington giggle. I moved faster.

Suddenly I was sliding, reaching for anything to grab. I smacked into a tree. That slowed me down. I threw my arms around another one and stopped.

Careful, I told myself. *Safety is more important than speed.*

The slope in front of me was too steep and slippery. I had to go back up some and try again. This spot was way too dangerous.

The soldiers were waiting up above. They sang louder. I didn't care. There wasn't anything they could do to hurt me.

The walking had warmed me some. Sweat was dripping down my face, which was scratched from tree branches. My arms and legs felt bruised.

I went much slower now. I knew I must be at least halfway down the mountain. As long as I could keep from breaking a leg—or worse—I'd be off this mountain in an hour.

So I stopped after every few steps and looked around. I tested the ground ahead with a foot to make sure it was sturdy. I swept the weak light in a circle, checking for cliffs or steep ledges.

Worthington kept giggling. I did my best to ignore him. He sounded far away, but I knew he was watching me. He might do something bad any time.

Even though I was ready for the worst, Worthington's next move surprised me.

Suddenly he was on the trail in front of me, glowing brighter than before.

"You'll never make it back without my help!" he said.

"I don't need your help."

"You're heading straight for the cliff," he said. "I sent those soldiers to stop you."

I laughed, even though I was afraid. "You sent them to trick me. They would have led me over the cliff."

Worthington's glow began to fade. He looked tired and sad. "You'll end up like me," he said.

I checked my gut again. Something told me he was trying to help me.

"Which way?" I asked.

He pointed. "The cliff is right over there," he said. "You were heading straight toward it. The way down isn't easy from here, but the worst parts are behind you."

"Show me," I said.

"I can't." Worthington had faded so much I could barely see him. "My energy is all used up for tonight," he said. And then he disappeared.

I was finally alone. Bruised, cold, scared, and alone.

"Mom!" I called. My voice was as weak as the flashlight. I stood still for several minutes. Then I walked. If Worthington was being honest, I'd avoid the cliff. If he was lying, I'd probably fall to my death.

There was no ground under my next footstep! Was this the cliff?

I dropped, hit a smooth rock, and protected my head with my hands.

The steep drop wasn't far. I rolled into a tree and grasped for anything. But I kept sliding.

I slid at least twenty feet, scratching my hands and skinning both knees. I crashed to a stop in a thicket of bushes, wet and bleeding but without any breaks or sprains.

Somehow my flashlight had fallen all the way with me. I reached as far as I could and grabbed it.

I let out my breath in a giant sigh. I'd survived. This wasn't the cliff, but it was a very steep bank.

Something fluttered in the leaves above me. A small creature hopped along the thin branches.

Chip-a-whee.

Did I know that sound?

Chip-a-whee.

I shined the light up and around. It came to rest on a small, yellow bird.

The white-eyed vireo.

"Mom! Dad!" I yelled.

I waited a moment. Then yelled again.

"We're coming, Max!" Mom called back. She sounded far away, but I didn't care. They were on their way!

"Stay where you are!" Dad yelled.

My yelling scared the bird. It was gone. They'd be sorry they missed it, but I knew I'd be a better sight anyway.

"Over here!" I hollered. "Over here!"

This horrible day was ending.

I'd made it down the mountain.

ENDING

→» 3 «←

Stalking Woe

"Go away," I said to Worthington. "I wouldn't follow you anywhere."

Of course, my plan was to do exactly that. I'd let him think I was taking my own route, but I'd do my best to keep him in sight. If I was quiet and stayed hidden, he'd lead me back to Aunt Ida's house without realizing it.

If he knew I was following him, he would probably take me to the cliff he'd fallen from. Everything he'd done so far had been mean. It seemed all along he wanted to destroy me. I think he was jealous because I had my whole life ahead of me. His had been cut short by disaster.

"I'm staying right here until someone finds me," I said. "My parents will come looking soon."

"They'll never find you at night," Worthington said. "You'll freeze to death."

I shook my head. "Get lost," I told him. "I'm not moving another inch."

That made him laugh. "I'm not the lost one," he said. "Suit yourself. I'm going home."

He started along the path. I watched until the greenish glow was nearly out of sight. Then I took a few careful steps to follow.

It looked as if I had outsmarted him.

Now I had two big concerns. I had to be careful not to fall, and I had to keep Worthington in sight. I also had to make sure he didn't know I was behind him.

He was moving very quickly. Soon I couldn't see him at all.

He'd led me partway, but my plan was spoiled. Still, I was no worse off than before. If I kept going down, I would eventually be off the mountain. I'd probably reach a road. But my plan to follow Worthington had ended too quickly.

I tried to find a landmark. Nothing looked familiar. My flashlight beam gave off very little light. I could see only a short way in front of me, and only along the ground.

Should I yell? Or would that bring Worthington back?

He probably knew exactly where I was anyway. So I yelled.

"Mom! Dad!"

Nothing.

I sat on a boulder to rest. I hadn't seen a trail in a long time. Mostly I had been sliding downhill on the rocks or inching my way along by grabbing a tree and moving to the next one. It was almost impossible to stay on my feet. Every part of my legs and arms was cut or bruised.

But I'd get there. I started again.

My hands were bleeding from the tree bark and branches. My sweatshirt was torn in a couple of places, too.

In a few minutes I saw Worthington down below. He was moving at a steady pace, and he didn't look my way. I stood still for a minute and watched him. It seemed certain he didn't know I was there.

My instinct told me he was getting close to Aunt Ida's house.

So I tried to follow him again.

And I tripped.

My knee banged a rock on the way down. I didn't hurt it bad, but my pants tore and I skinned my knee. My hands hit hard, but they caught on solid rock. I pushed myself up and took a deep breath. My flashlight was a few feet below. If I lost that, I'd be sunk.

I could still see Worthington. The path he was following must have been winding, because he seemed to be circling his way down. I did my best to keep up. It wasn't easy. This was the hardest thing I'd ever done, in fact.

We reached a flat area. *We must be close to home,* I thought. *Safety! Warmth! Food!*

There was an opening in the woods just ahead. I felt a surge of energy. Had we made it? Was this the clearing by Aunt Ida's house?

Worthington was still walking. I went faster.

But that was my big mistake! Woe could float across open space. I couldn't!

I hit hard on my shoulder and rolled down a very steep rocky slope, grabbing at branches to try to stop myself. Pain shot through my ankle.

I skidded to a stop, gripping hard on a scrubby bush.

Worthington giggled. He was floating in space, twenty feet in front of me.

Where was I? I had fallen several feet and was lucky I hadn't hit my head. My flashlight was gone.

"Welcome to the cliff," Worthington said.

My ankle was throbbing and I was all scratched up, but things could have been much worse. Gradually I was able to see better as my eyes adjusted to the moonlight. I was perched on a narrow, flat area, just above a gaping drop. Above me was the spot from which I'd fallen. I guessed I was ten feet below it.

I couldn't see Worthington anymore, but I knew he must be smiling. He'd tricked me. He'd led me over the cliff after all. Only luck had kept me from falling all the way, as he had done fifty years before.

I should have stayed on the mountain and waited to be rescued. I would have been cold and wet and scared, but now I was all of those things. And hurt. I touched my ankle but it felt like it was on fire. Just a gentle poke from my finger sent pain shooting up my leg.

There was no way I could climb back up. I was stuck here until someone found me.

"Congratulations, Worthington," I said. "You almost killed me. But the joke's on you. My parents will rescue me. I know they will."

Worthington laughed again.

Maybe he knew better than I did.

I screamed as loud as I could for the next five minutes.

The only reply was Worthington's giggles. His laughter grew fainter as he floated away.

This was going to be the longest night of my life. All I could do was hold on until morning.

But I'm still alive to tell this story.

Because I did it.

Write Your Own Ending

There were three endings to choose from in *The Room of Woe*. Did you find the ending you wanted from the story? Or did you want something different to happen? Now it is your turn! Write the ending you would like to see. Be creative!